Supported by

"This is a story that must be told and sharing it through the lens of the sea turtle is especially powerful. We can all do our part to make the ocean and beaches cleaner and Sheldon is our inspiration."
Dr. Mikki McComb-Kobza, Executive Director, Ocean First institute, www.oceanfirstinstitute.org

"This book highlights the plight of our marine mammals. Refusing, reducing, reusing and recycling plastics and participating in beach cleans and litter picks wherever you are can help protect our ocean planet."
Lizzi Larbalestier: Blue Health Coach, BDMLR Marine Mammal Medic and SAS Rep.
www.goingcoastal.blue

"Plastic pollution and ocean waste are a growing problem. This book highlights how everyone can contribute to the protection of our marine environment and beaches and in doing so leave no trace."
Leave No Trace Ireland. www.leavenotraceireland.org

"REEF conserves marine environments worldwide by actively engaging and inspiring the public through citizen science, education and partnerships with the scientific community. This book is a good reminder that each of us can take action to support healthy oceans."
Martha Klitzkie, Director of Operations, Reef Environmental Education Foundation (REEF)
www.REEF.org

"Everyone needs to know and care about their neighbours, even when their neighbours are other species, living in other neighbourhoods. And as this book shows - our neighbours often are other species living close enough to feel the things we are doing."
Carl Safina, Author and Ecologist. www.safinacenter.org

"The key to cleaning the ocean is education of our children, the future. We at RECOVER appreciate all efforts made to educate our children, this book is a fun and exciting way to do this very thing."
Jefferson Jackson, President RECOVER (Restore Earth's Clean Ocean with Versatile Ersatz Reef).
www.ersatzreef.org

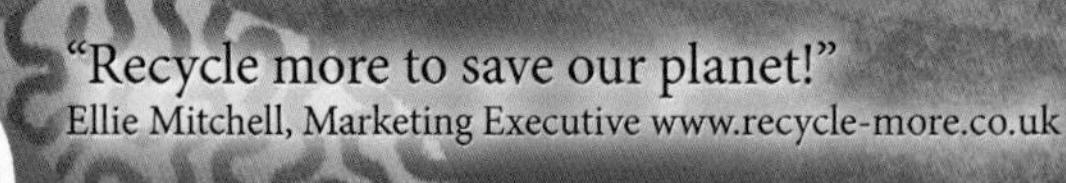

"Recycle more to save our planet!"
Ellie Mitchell, Marketing Executive www.recycle-more.co.uk

Turtle Trouble

Written by Stuart McDonald

Published by Amazon KDP 2019

Illustrations by Rosalia Destarisa

ISBN: 9781686321894

Sheldon was a turtle teen,
and always up to tricks.
Forever swimming too far off,
or getting in a fix.

His parents kept on telling him,
"Stay closer to the shore."
But Sheldon's an adventurer.
He just wants to explore!

One day, just after turtle school,
Sheldon was swimming home.
He noticed something glistening,
amongst the briny foam.
He swam on over closer,
to see what it could be.
But a current took a hold of him
and swept him out to sea!

He fought to swim against it,
but the ocean was too strong.
Further out it took him still.
He knew this was all wrong!

The current pulled him round
the coast, into a sheltered bay.
His chance to reach the shore,
he thought? But sadly not that day.

The bay was full of washed up waste, with bottles, bags and more.
Rubbish tossed into the sea, or just dropped on the floor.

Sheldon's flippers got caught up, inside some plastic junk.
He really needed to break free, or soon he would be sunk!

He was getting tired now. His energy was low.
The water pushed and pulled at him, with each ebb and flow.
A boy was fishing off the rocks and spotted the commotion.
He quickly dropped his fishing gear and dived into the ocean!

The boy swam Sheldon back to shore
and cut his flippers loose!
Untangling him from all those bags,
wrapped round him like a noose.

The boy took Sheldon round the bay
and placed him in the sea.
Somewhere safe and clear of junk,
where Sheldon could swim free.

He swam back home to tell his tale,
but that's not how this ends...

The boy went home and the next day recruited all his friends.

The whole town took their fishing boats and tidied up the bay.
They formed a seaside cleaning group and go there every day.

The story made the front page news.
Signs went up all around.
"Please pick up your litter.
Don't just drop it on the ground!"

The beach is really tidy now.
The bay is free of waste.
So remember, please recycle.
Make this world a cleaner place.

Other books by Stuart McDonald

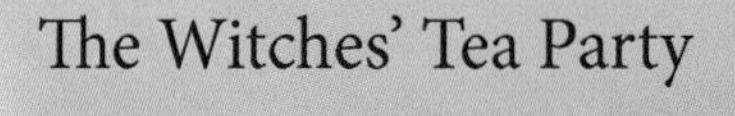

The Witches' Tea Party

Heggerty Witch is having a tea party and has five hard-to-please friends to impress! What spooktacular food will she rustle up from her small kitchenette? Will her guests behave themselves? Will they even like the food?

Special Thanks

I'd like to say a HUGE thank you to the organisations who very kindly supported this book and also provided those wonderful quotes, which will only help to further underline the importance of this story.

For more information please visit their websites:
www.oceanfirstinstitute.org
www.goingcoastal.blue
www.leavenotraceireland.org
www.REEF.org
www.safinacenter.org
www.ersatzreef.org
www.recycle-more.co.uk

Lastly, I would like to thank all my family, friends and readers, who continue to support me with all of my writing.

To find out how you can make a difference and do your bit to help the environment, turn the page...

Sheldon's checklist to help save our planet:

- ✔ Reduce, Reuse, Recycle! But do it right. Visit the websites on the inside page for more information.
- ✔ Reduce the amount of plastics you buy.
- ✔ Buy more unpackaged/plastic-free products.
- ✔ Never litter! Always find a bin or take it home.
- ✔ Stop buying bottled water. Refill your own reusable bottle.
  Two thirds of plastic water bottles are never recycled!
- ✔ Refill your bottle when you're out and about. Don't be shy to ask at cafes, restaurants, garages etc.
  They're always happy to help.
- ✔ Say NO to plastic straws (and even paper ones). Buy a reusable stainless steel one.
- ✔ Don't forget to reuse your shopping bags. Most supermarkets offer free replacements
  on damaged bags and will recycle your old ones.
- ✔ Stop using wipes, which contain plastic and are difficult to recycle.
- ✔ Choose loose, unpackaged fruit, veg and other items, when there's an option.
- ✔ At your next party, avoid paper plates, plastic straws, cups and cutlery.
- ✔ Find and join a local beach or park cleaning group or ask your school to organise a litter pick.
- ✔ Listen to Jack Johnson's song "Reduce, Reuse, Recycle" (The 3 R's").

Printed in Great Britain
by Amazon